This book belongs to:

- - - - - - - - - - - - -

Characters

Mr. Koala and Mr. Cat are talking about the competition.

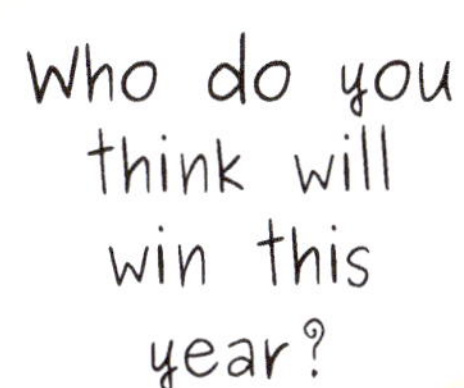

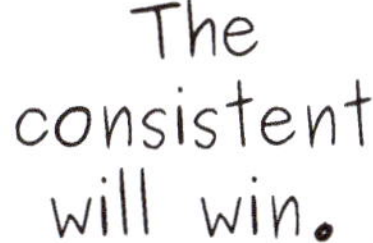

I will carry my plant wherever I go. I will water it all day long until the competition day.

Few days later!

She will never win if she will wait for the rain.
These are the Rain Flowers. They grow colorful flowers whenever it rains.
These are the most beautiful flowers I've ever seen!

Thank you beautiful Clouds for being so generous. My beautiful Rain Flowers you look amazing.

Mr. Panda decided to quit his workouts and so he ate a lot of bamboo leaves. He fell asleep until the competition day.

Mr. Panda

Mr. Chick stopped currying his plant. He also remembered that he didn't water it for days. Mr. Chick felt sorry but he soon forgot about the plant and went on a very long walk in the park.

Ms. Rosey was very consistent. She kept on watering and caring for her Flowers that they grew bigger and bigger each day. They also became more colorful and every one in the town was talking about how beautiful they smelt.

On The Competition Day
Ms. Rosey brought her beautiful
flowers and she won the copetition.
Well done! Ms. Rosey.
Your hard work and
consistency were the key
to your success.
Mr. Coala

Your Journey Starts Here

What do you learn from the story?! Illustrate then write

Now Your Turn
To Write Your Own Story

Instructions

It's time to write your own story! Illustrating your scenes and characters will be fun if you share with a sibling or a friend.

To build scenes, use your own imagination.

Add characters and imagine a situation where they face challenges.

Enjoy illustrating and writing text as you go to build your story.

Happy writing!

Where did your story happen? Illustrate the scene then write a sentence to describe it.

Who is the main character? Illustrate the character then write about its role in the story.

Who else in your story? Illustrate the characters then write about their roles in the story. Choose 3 characters.

Now start telling your story. What happens with your characters?! Illustrate then write

What happens next?! Illustrate then write

What are your characters discussing about?
Illustrate then write

Your story is about to reach its end. What is happening now?! Illustrate then write

What happens to your charcaters at the end of the story?
Illustrate then write

Well done young writer! You have written your own story. Can you please tell us about the moral you have learnt from your own story? Illustrate then write

Well Done!